"**Jill Murphy deserves a constellation of gold stars for consistently writing picture books that please children and enrapture parents.**" *Observer*

When Jill Murphy penned the first of the Large Family series over 30 years ago, little did she know that her elephants would speak to so many, the stories going on to sell over five million copies worldwide. Today, numerous awards and a television adaptation later, they ring as true as ever, and continue to be celebrated for their beautifully observed depiction of hectic, warm – but ultimately ordinary – family life.

THIS BOOK BELONGS TO:

....

First published 1989 by Walker Books Ltd
87 Vauxhall Walk, London SE11 5HJ

This edition published 2017

2 4 6 8 10 9 7 5 3 1

This book has been typeset in Bembo Educational

Printed in China

British Library Cataloguing in Publication Data:
a catalogue record for this book is available from the British Library

ISBN 978-1-4063-7073-7

www.walker.co.uk

A Piece of Cake

Jill Murphy

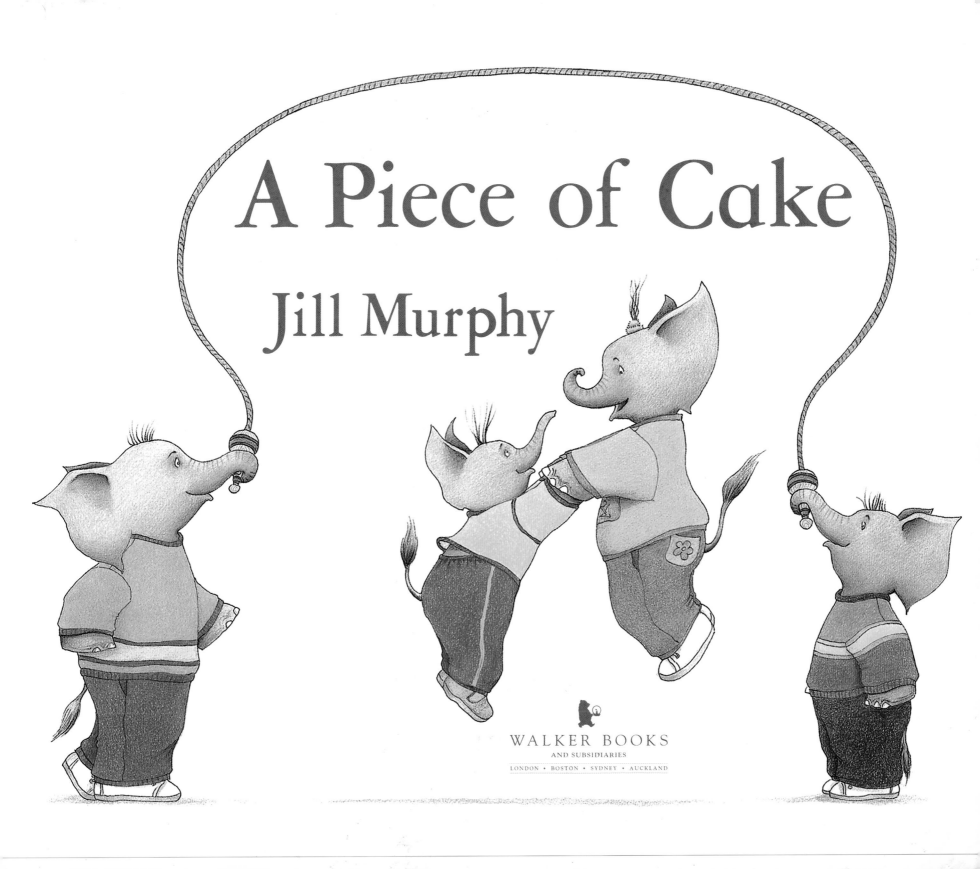

WALKER BOOKS
AND SUBSIDIARIES
LONDON • BOSTON • SYDNEY • AUCKLAND

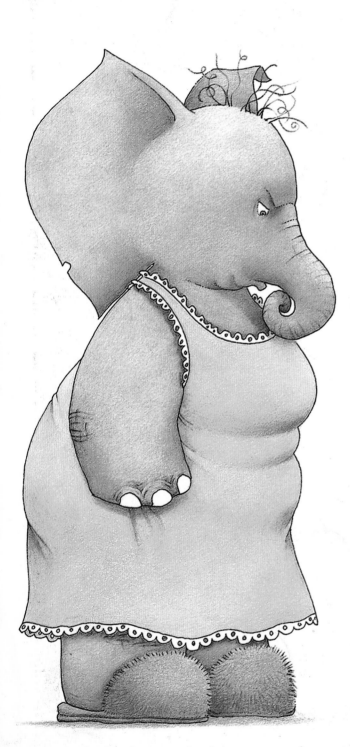

"I'm fat," said Mrs Large.

"No you're not," said Lester.

"You're our cuddly mummy,"
 said Laura.

"You're *just* right," said Luke.

"Mummy's got wobbly bits,"
 said the baby.

"Exactly," said Mrs Large. "As I was
 saying – I'm fat."

"We must all go on a diet," said Mrs Large.
"No more cakes. No more biscuits. No more
crisps. No more sitting around all day.
From now on, it's healthy living."

"Can we watch TV?" asked Lester, as they
trooped in from school.
"Certainly not!" said Mrs Large. "We're all
off for a nice healthy jog round the park."
And they were.

"What's for tea, Mum?" asked Laura
when they arrived home.

"Some nice healthy watercress soup," said
Mrs Large. "Followed by a nice healthy cup
of water."

"Oh!" said Laura. "That sounds ... nice."

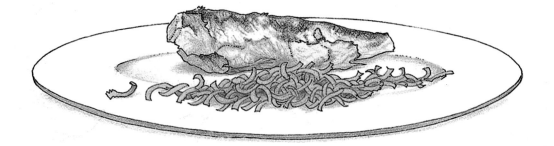

"I'm just going to watch the news, dear,"
  said Mr Large when he came home from work.
"No you're not, dear," said Mrs Large.
"You're off for a nice healthy jog round
  the park, followed by your tea – a delicious
  sardine with grated carrot."
"I can't wait," said Mr Large.

It was awful. Every morning there was a healthy breakfast followed by exercises. Then there was a healthy tea followed by a healthy jog.

By the time evening came everyone felt terrible.

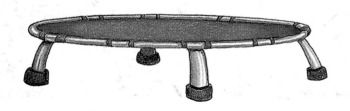

"We aren't getting any thinner, dear,"
  said Mr Large.

"Perhaps elephants are *meant* to be fat,"
  said Luke.

"Nonsense!" said Mrs Large. "We mustn't
  give up now."

"Wibbly-wobbly, wibbly-wobbly," went
  the baby.

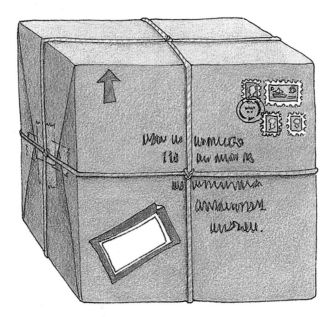

One morning a parcel arrived. It was a cake from Granny. Everyone stared at it hopefully. Mrs Large put it into the cupboard on a high shelf. "Just in case we have visitors," she said sternly.

Everyone kept thinking about the cake.
They thought about it during tea. They
thought about it during the healthy jog.
They thought about it in bed that night.
Mrs Large sat up. "I can't stand it any
more," she said to herself. "I must have
a piece of that cake."

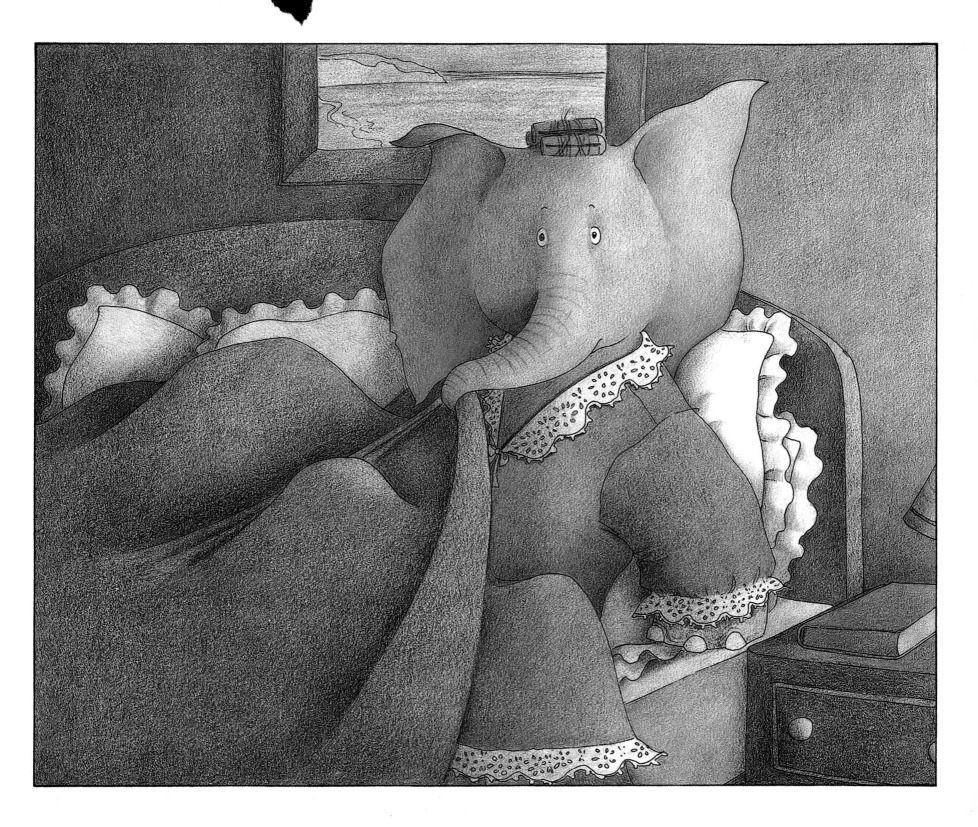

Mrs Large crept out of bed and went
downstairs to the kitchen. She took a knife
out of the drawer and opened the cupboard.
There was only one piece of cake left!

"Ah ha!" said Mr Large, seeing the knife.
"Caught in the act!"
   Mrs Large switched on the light and saw
   Mr Large and all the children hiding
   under the table.
"There *is* one piece left," said Laura in
   a helpful way.

Mrs Large began to laugh. "We're all as bad as each other!" she said, eating the last piece of cake before anyone else did.

"I do think elephants are meant to be fat," said Luke.

"I think you're probably right, dear," said Mrs Large.

"Wibbly-wobbly, wibbly-wobbly!" went the baby.

JILL MURPHY

is one of Britain's most treasured author-illustrators, who created her first book, the bestselling *The Worst Witch*, while still only eighteen. She is best known for her award-winning Large Family series – a series which includes *Five Minutes' Peace,* the Kate Greenaway commended *All in One Piece,* and the shortlisted *A Quiet Night In.* Among Jill's very popular characters are a small monster called Marlon, who appears in the acclaimed picture books *The Last Noo-Noo* and *All For One,* and Ruby the bunny, who stars in *Meltdown!*

Jill lives in Cornwall.